# Dear Parents:

Congratulations! Your child is taking the first steps on an exciting journey. The destination? Independent reading!

**STEP INTO READING**® will help your child get there. The program offers five steps to reading success. Each step includes fun stories and colorful art or photographs. In addition to original fiction and books with favorite characters, there are Step into Reading Non-Fiction Readers, Phonics Readers and Boxed Sets, Sticker Readers, and Comic Readers—a complete literacy program with something to interest every child.

## Learning to Read, Step by Step!

### Ready to Read   Preschool–Kindergarten
• big type and easy words • rhyme and rhythm • picture clues
For children who know the alphabet and are eager to begin reading.

### Reading with Help   Preschool–Grade 1
• basic vocabulary • short sentences • simple stories
For children who recognize familiar words and sound out new words with help.

### Reading on Your Own   Grades 1–3
• engaging characters • easy-to-follow plots • popular topics
For children who are ready to read on their own.

### Reading Paragraphs   Grades 2–3
• challenging vocabulary • short paragraphs • exciting stories
For newly independent readers who read simple sentences with confidence.

### Ready for Chapters   Grades 2–4
• chapters • longer paragraphs • full-color art
For children who want to take the plunge into chapter books but still like colorful pictures.

**STEP INTO READING**® is designed to give every child a successful reading experience. The grade levels are only guides; children will progress through the steps at their own speed, developing confidence in their reading.

Remember, a lifetime love of reading starts with a single step!

Visit us on the Web!
StepIntoReading.com
rhcbooks.com

Educators and librarians, for a variety of teaching tools, visit us at RHTeachersLibrarians.com

ISBN 978-0-525-57814-7 (trade) — ISBN 978-0-525-57815-4 (lib. bdg.)

Printed in the United States of America   10 9 8 7 6 5 4 3 2 1

Sunny Day

# STICK WITH ME!

adapted by Courtney Carbone

based on the teleplay by Alison Greenaway

illustrated by Susan Hall

Random House 🏠 New York

Sunny's Salon is open.
A ballet dancer
named Hannah visits.

She needs her hair
to be put in
a fancy bun.

Sunny uses
super-sticky
hair spray.
It is <u>very</u> sticky!

The dancer invites
Sunny and her friends
to the ballet.

Oh, no!

The super-sticky hair spray gets on Rox and Blair.

They are stuck together!

How can Rox and Blair
get unstuck?
Sunny knows!

She needs to mix
crab apples, sugar,
salt, and water.

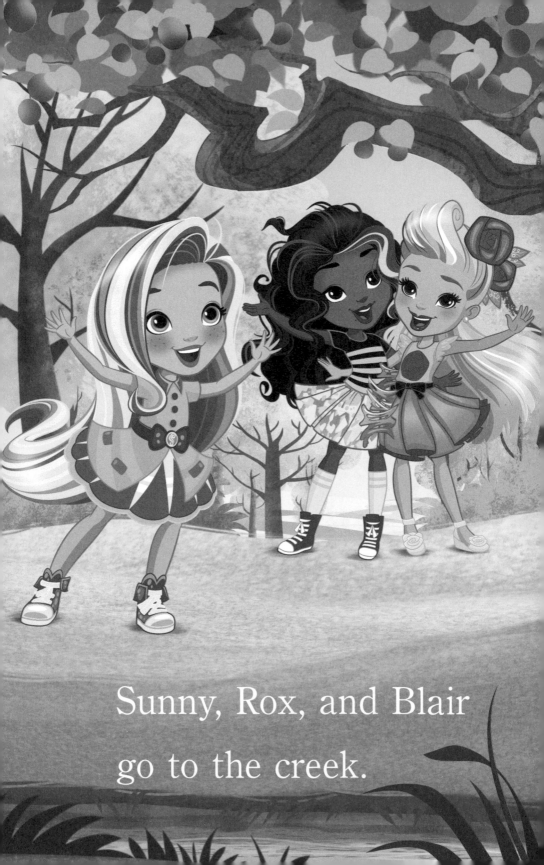

Sunny, Rox, and Blair

go to the creek.

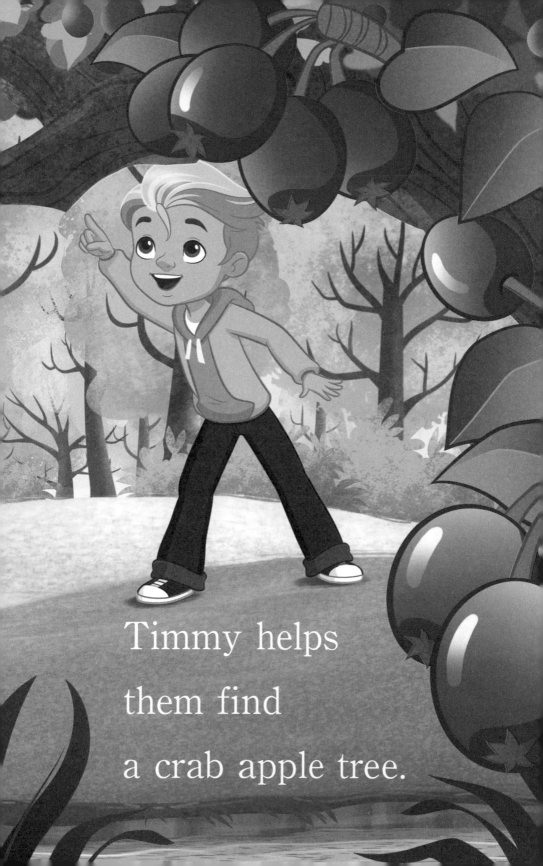

Timmy helps
them find
a crab apple tree.

Next, they go
to the bakery.

Cindy the baker

has sugar.

But she is out of salt.

Sunny has an idea!

They drive to the beach.

They can get salt
and water
from the sea!

18

Uh-oh!
Now the hair spray
gets on Sunny.
Her hands stick
to the pier!

Rox and Blair
work together.
They mix
the crab apples,
sugar, salt, and water.

It works!

They are all unstuck!

They get to the ballet
just in time.

The dancing is
wonderful.

It is a sunny day
when friends
stick together!